Get in the Game! With Robin Roberts

Sports

INJURIES

The Millbrook Press   Brookfield, Connecticut

The author and publisher wish to thank Bill Gutman for his research and writing contributions to this series.

Published by The Millbrook Press, Inc.
2 Old New Milford Road
Brookfield, Connecticut 06804
www.millbrookpress.com

Cover photograph courtesy of Steve Fenn/ABC

Photographs courtesy of Allsport: pp. 1 (© Robert Cianflone), 30 (© Scott Halleran); © Patrick Flynn: p. 4; Photo Edit, Inc.: pp. 8 (© Rudi Von Briel), 10 (© Tony Freeman), 17 (© Michael Newman), 21 (© Will Hart); Corbis: p. 14 (© Jack Hollingsworth); Stock Boston: pp. 23 (© A. Ramey), 42 (© Bob Daemmrich); SportsChrome USA: p. 32 (© Brian Drake); Photo Researchers, Inc.: p. 38 (© Carolyn A. McKeone)

Library of Congress Cataloging-in-Publication Data
Roberts, Robin, 1960-
Sports injuries : how to stay safe and keep on playing / Robin Roberts.
p. cm. –(Get in the game! With Robin Roberts)
Includes index.
ISBN 0-7613-2116-0 (lib. bdg.). — 0-7613-1449-0 (pbk)
1. Sports injuries—Juvenile literature. 2. Sports injuries in children—Juvenile literature. [1. Sports injuries.] I. Title.
RD97 .R634 2001
617.1'027—dc21   00-068096

CONTENTS

Introduction

Sports has always been a big part of my life. From playing sandlot football with the other kids in my neighborhood in Biloxi, Mississippi, to playing tennis in high school and basketball in college, to working in sports broadcasting at ESPN, I can't imagine my life without sports. It used to be that girls who played sports were labeled "tomboys." These days, however, women and sports go hand-in-hand in so many ways.

Sports can increase a girl's confidence and help her to feel good about herself, and can help her succeed in nearly every aspect of life including school, a career, and relationships with friends and family.

With **Get in the Game!** my goal is to share my love and knowledge of the world of sports, and to show just how important sports can be. What you can learn on the field, court, rink, and arena are ways to solve problems, communicate with others, and become a leader. No matter what your skill level, if you learn all that sports can teach you, how can you *not* succeed at life in general? And the best part is that, like I have, you'll have fun at the same time!

—Robin Roberts

Sooner or later, everyone who participates in sports regularly will suffer an injury. That's a fact of sporting life. Millions of girls and boys play sports such as soccer, basketball, softball, and baseball, or compete in tennis, swimming, volleyball, gymnastics, track, and cross-country each year. Some sports require more physical contact than others. All of them, however, can lead to injuries.

The numbers can be staggering. Statistics show that more than 4 million sports-related injuries occur among people from age 5 to 17 each year. More than 1 million of them are considered serious. A partial breakdown by sport shows more than 1 million injuries in basketball, some 900,000 in baseball, 500,000 in football, 110,000 in gymnastics, and 105,000 in soccer. That doesn't include the other sports, as well as recreational activities such as skateboarding, bicycling, and in-line skating.

Learning how to cope with an injury is a part of being an athlete. You must also know how to prepare and compete in a way that will minimize your chances of getting hurt. If you do get hurt, you must recognize the injury and report it to your athletic trainer, coach, or parents immediately. Don't assume that an injury isn't serious and continue to play. Always get yourself checked out. Many doctors specialize in sports medicine, and many schools employ athletic trainers. They can evaluate an injury and instruct you on the best way to treat it. They will also let you know when you can safely begin to play again.

This book will detail a variety of sports injuries, how they happen, how you can recognize and treat them, and what you can do to try to prevent them. The fear of injury should not stop anyone from playing a sport. The benefits of sports to your mental and physical health are important, too. Injuries are simply part of the game. The more you know about injuries, the better equipped you will be to handle them when they happen.

Girls and boys have differing physical characteristics that can make them perform differently at sports and be susceptible to different sports injuries.

The Differences Between Girls and Boys

There was a time when most sports were deemed too difficult for girls. Girls weren't strong enough, people said. Girls didn't have enough endurance, weren't built for physical contact, and couldn't learn the same advanced skills as boys. It wasn't until the 1970s, for instance, that girls were allowed to play the same brand of full-court basketball played by boys. Many people thought that girls didn't have the stamina to run up and down the court at full speed. Now we know that isn't true.

In fact, almost every barrier to women's sports has been broken. Girls and women play nearly every sport that boys and men play. Many play them extremely well. The increasing number of girls playing sports and playing them hard, however, has also caused a rapid rise in sports-related injuries among girls.

Most agree that, in general, the injury rates for female athletes are no higher than those for males. However, some physical differences in girls and women make them more likely to suffer certain types of sports injuries than their male counterparts.

One serious injury that is prevalent in girls is a tear of the anterior cruciate ligament (ACL) in the knee. The ACL is a band of tissue that helps control the movement of the knee. The injury usually occurs in

Field hockey is another sport that involves fast stops and starts, which can increase the likelihood of an ACL injury.

sports such as basketball or soccer that require pivoting as well as fast stops and starts. One study of college athletes found that female basketball players were three times more likely to sustain a tear of the ACL as male basketball players. Women suffered ACL injuries in soccer at a rate twice that of the men.

Another study, taking in all sports, had the numbers even higher. It said that female athletes were tearing knee ligaments at a rate six to ten times that of men! Why the difference? There are several theories. Dr. Gary Wadler, a sports-medicine specialist and vice president of the Women's Sports Foundation, believes that women's wider hips may put additional strain on the knee joint. Sports physician Dr. Ralph Gambardella has said that "the angle of the knee is a little dif-

ferent in a female because of the pelvis." These physical characteristics of women may account for their increased risk of knee injuries.

Another theory is that girls and women beginning to play sports may not be properly strengthening their lower bodies. Athletic trainer Sarah Scott feels that girls should focus on building muscle in areas most susceptible to wear and tear—the ankles, knees, and lower back, since young female athletes seem to have more lower-body injuries.

Medical studies have also shown that female athletes experience more stress fractures than their male counterparts. A stress fracture is a tiny crack in a bone occurring when muscles become fatigued and are unable to absorb added shock. Most stress fractures occur in the weight-bearing bones of the lower leg and foot. Although the evidence hasn't fully been established, many orthopedic surgeons feel that eating disorders (bulimia and anorexia), amenorrhea (infrequent menstrual cycle), and osteoporosis (loss of bone mass) are contributing factors. The first two can affect young girls; the third usually affects older women. All should be a concern for female athletes.

What is true for both girls and boys is that any reckless athlete will be more prone to injury. An athlete who doesn't train properly will also be more prone to injury. And an athlete who doesn't report an injury will be prone to a more serious injury.

It is important that every athlete be aware of the types of injury she might suffer and how to handle it when she does, as well as how to prevent injuries in the first place.

How Do You Know When Something Is Wrong?

No one who competes in athletics on a regular basis is going to feel great all the time. Even if you are in top shape, you will be sore at times, have bumps and bruises, and aches and pains. This is especially true if you are involved in a contact sport such as basketball or soccer. Even if you train very hard at an individual sport such as track or swimming, there will be times when your body talks back.

As an athlete, you must know your body. You must learn to judge which aches and pains may need medical attention, and which may indicate a serious injury. At the same time, you must learn how to treat everyday soreness while continuing to practice and play.

For example, you can expect to have muscle soreness when you haven't exercised for some time or are trying a new exercise or training method. In each case, you are using muscles in a way they haven't been used in a while. This creates micro-scopic tears in the connective tissues in your body. Although this sounds serious, it is a natural response of the muscles.

It is also a reason to make sure that you have enough rest between workouts. An athlete training with weights, for example, gets these tiny tears in the muscle each time she works outs. With rest, the muscles rebuild and become even bigger and stronger. Without rest, the tears con-tinue to multiply and can lead to a real injury.

Repeated contractions of mus-cles during a strenuous weight work-out can also cause pain. This type of pain is caused by lactic and other acids, as well as proteins and hor-mones, building up in muscle tissue. This is also normal pain without injury. Once you rest, the pain should subside. However, if you have a sharp, continuous pain, or pain accompanied by a burning sen-

A good rest between weight workouts decreases the risk of injury and also makes workouts more effective.

sation, stop the workout and see an athletic trainer or doctor.

Cramps are another normal by-product of some workouts. A cramp occurs when a muscle, often in the calves or feet, knots up in intense contractions. Cramps are most common in endurance sports such as cycling and running, and in high-exertion sports such as soccer and field hockey. They happen especially when the athlete loses a lot of fluids through sweating. A cramp is not a serious injury, and can be gently stretched out. In the future, it can be avoided by taking in more fluids before and during a workout.

Even when you exercise regularly, you may have some muscle soreness during and right after your workout. This is caused by fatigue and a buildup of the chemical waste products of exercise. This type of soreness or discomfort will often go away after you rest just a few minutes. Then you can continue to exercise without any lasting effects. Of course, if the pain persists, then more rest or a visit to the doctor is suggested.

Many young athletes have various aches and pains that are described as growing pains—the result of young bodies continuing to grow in size and strength. One type of growing pain should be taken seriously. It is caused by repetitive stress during running, jumping, and other activities involving motions in the knee. It is called Osgood-Schlatter disease and is quite common in growing athletes, although a bit more common in boys than in girls. Repetitive stress may cause inflammation and pain in the tendon of the knee and may result in an enlargement or swelling just below the kneecap.

If you feel you have this problem, you can continue to participate in sports if the pain doesn't become too severe. If it does, rest is prescribed. You should also use ice after you work out, and do lots of stretching to help the condition. Once an athlete stops growing, Osgood-Schlatter disease disappears.

All athletes, especially those in contact sports, will get their share of bumps and bruises. Most of these bruises are minor, and you can continue playing as they heal. A more serious bruise, or contusion, will cause some internal bleeding, as well as swelling, pain, and stiffness. A contusion can be very painful and might even put you out of action for a few days. Despite this, it is rarely a serious injury.

In this section, we have discussed some of the normal kinds of soreness and minor injuries that are part of every young athlete's life. There are, however, certain general signs and symptoms that your injury isn't minor. When these signs appear, be sure to tell your coach and your parents, and make sure you see a doctor or athletic trainer before continuing with your sport.

- Any sharp or burning pain that does not subside in a short time
- Any pain or tightness in an arm, shoulder, wrist, hand, foot, knee, or leg that restricts your movement or ability to put pressure on that body part
- Any feeling of dizziness, light-headedness, or nausea following a blow to the head or an intense workout in the heat
- Any sharp, tearing pain in the leg area after a quick, explosive movement

Repetitive stress on the knees, such as from running and jumping, can promote Osgood-Schlatter disease in young athletes.

- Intense pain in the ankle or knee after jumping and landing awkwardly
- Any type of bruise or other seemingly minor injury that doesn't heal in the time it should

There are other specific warning signs of serious injury. Some, such as a broken bone, or fracture, are obvious and should not be ignored. A compound fracture, in which part of the broken bone protrudes through the skin, is the most serious of all. The severe, burning pain of any fracture, however, should not be ignored and requires immediate medical attention.

Several general injuries can affect different parts of the body. The most common of these are sprains and strains. A *sprain* is a stretched or torn ligament. It occurs most often in ankles, knees, wrists, or fingers. A *strain* is a stretched or torn muscle or tendinous attachment. Symptoms are similar for both injuries, and include pain or tenderness in the area of injury; swelling in the affected joint; redness or bruising in the area of injury, immediately or several hours after the initial injury; and loss of normal movement in the injured joint.

With injuries such as sprains and strains, you may feel you can ignore the pain and keep playing. That could be a big mistake. When in doubt about the seriousness of an injury, always check with an athletic trainer or doctor.

R.I.C.E.

The best method for treating strains and sprains is one that an athlete will hear about quite often. It is called R.I.C.E. therapy, and it has nothing to do with food. R.I.C.E. stands for Rest, Ice, Compression, and Elevation. Rest is simply an immediate stop to using the muscle, bone, or joint that hurts. Ice should be applied to the injured area within twenty-four hours. Place the ice in a plastic bag and separate it from the skin with a thin towel. Keep the ice pack on the injured area for up to two hours at a time, constantly or intermittently, depending on how you can tolerate the cold. Continue at two-hour intervals for twenty-four hours.

After twenty-four hours you may continue the ice or switch to heat. Some doctors feel that ice should be continued for forty-eight hours before the switch. But never use heat during the first twenty-four hours after the injury. This could increase bleeding and swelling and lengthen the healing time.

Whenever possible, the injury should be wrapped with an elastic bandage or special sleeve that compresses the joint. Compression helps reduce swelling. The injured area should also be raised, or elevated, whenever possible (especially when you are sleeping), so that fluid can drain and diminish swelling. By doing this, you are preventing blood from pooling at the injury site. These are the four important steps of R.I.C.E. therapy.

Overexertion and Head and Neck Injuries

Perhaps the most common of all sports-related problems are due to overexertion—not knowing when to stop. As fatigue overtakes the muscles, both strength and coordination decrease, leaving the tired athlete more prone to injury.

Young athletes should not be pushed to exhaustion and certainly not beyond it. A good coach is aware of this. That's why, in team sports, everyone should have a turn to play. By bringing in fresh players, no one player will be overexerted.

HEAT EXHAUSTION AND HEATSTROKE

Overexertion in high heat and humidity can cause an athlete to suffer either heat exhaustion or heatstroke. Both are considered serious injuries. Heat exhaustion is rarely life threatening. But if it goes unattended, it can lead to heat-stroke, which *is* life threatening. Both are caused by failure to properly hydrate the body (drink enough fluids) and, to a lesser degree, by not being acclimated to heat.

Symptoms of approaching heat exhaustion include headache, nausea, dizziness, lightheadedness, and a rapid pulse. If you begin to experience these symptoms while playing, you should stop immediately. Alert the coach or athletic trainer. Lie down in a shaded, cool area, but don't go into a cold place, such as an air-conditioned room, right away. You should then slowly sip water until the symptoms pass. You should not resume playing after suffering symptoms of heat exhaustion. Even if you feel better, wait until the next day to play again.

Precautions should be taken anytime you participate in sports in high heat, humidity, and strong sunlight.

Someone suffering from heatstroke begins showing symptoms of heat exhaustion, then becomes disoriented and eventually unconscious. Her body temperature becomes extremely high, usually above 104 degrees F (40 degrees C). First aid for heatstroke is cooling the victim's body as quickly as possible. This can sometimes mean immersing the person in cold water or rubbing her with alcohol. Because this is a life-threatening situation, any athlete suffering heatstroke should get medical attention as soon as possible. Even if the victim seems to be recovering, she should be checked out by a doctor.

Most cases of heat exhaustion and heatstroke can be prevented if both athletes and coach take some simple precautions. In hot, humid conditions, athletes lose a large amount of water during exercise through sweating. When this isn't replaced, they can suffer a heat-related problem. Athletes should always be sure to drink enough fluids before, during, and after their practice or exercise session.

Athletes should drink water regularly throughout the day. They should drink enough water so that they must urinate frequently and that their urine is clear. The most recent guidelines from the American College of Sports Medicine advise athletes to drink about 17 ounces (0.5 liter) of fluid two hours before exercise, then 5 to 12 ounces every 15 to 20 minutes during sports activity in the heat. Finally, the athlete must rehydrate after the workout. One good self-check is to weigh yourself before and after practice. If you weigh less after practice, it is because you have lost water. A rule of thumb is to drink about 16 ounces (1 pint) of fluid for every pound lost.

drate in the form of sugars (glucose or sucrose) or starch (maltodextrin). Many sports drinks contain these ratios.

Rehydrating the body with water or sports drinks is an easy way to guard against heat-related and other injuries.

Water is fine for those exercising an hour or less. New guidelines advise athletes involved in intense activity of more than an hour to drink a beverage containing some sodium plus 4 to 8 percent carbohy-

ACCLIMATE FIRST

Sports medicine specialist Greg Gutierrez confirms that "most heat illness occurs during the first days of training [in hot weather]." The reason is that the body has not acclimated to exercising in the hot weather. If possible, you should exercise for shorter periods and/or at lower intensity at first, gradually increasing the time and intensity as you begin to feel more comfortable. If you do this, your body will acclimate to the heat and humidity.

Try wearing lightweight, light-colored, and porous clothing during exercise. These will allow for the evaporation of sweat. If possible, avoid taping, padding, and nonessential equipment such as sweatbands, bandannas, and gloves. If you must wear a helmet, always remove it during breaks. Also, use a high-quality sunscreen on exposed areas of your body.

HEAD INJURIES

All head injuries incurred during a sports activity should be taken seriously. Research has shown that even seemingly minor head injuries can have effects years later. Perhaps the most common injury to the head is the concussion. It is caused by any jarring injury to the head, face, or jaw that results in a disturbance of the brain. Concussions are classified on a variety of levels, ranging from mild to severe. Any young athlete showing signs of concussion should be taken to a doctor immediately.

Symptoms of concussion can include any or all of the following: brief loss of consciousness, headache, grogginess, confusion, a glassy-eyed look, amnesia (loss of memory), disturbed balance, nausea, visual disturbances, ringing in the ears, and slight dizziness. Most concussions are mild, but the athlete should remain on the sidelines with an adult watching her closely to observe any change in behavior or additional symptoms. With evidence of a more severe concussion due to worsening symptoms, the athlete should be taken to the hospital immediately.

A young athlete must be completely free of all symptoms both while at rest and when exerting herself physically before returning to her sport. Mild concussions may require up to a week for recovery, with the final decision to play again made only by a doctor. A severe concussion may keep an athlete off the field for at least four weeks, with permission to return given only by a specialist in head injuries.

One word of caution: Research has indicated that so-called mild concussions might cause more brain damage than previously thought. One study indicated that head injuries that cause concussion can lead to changes that resemble the brain damage of a person in a coma. These changes, researchers say, can last for weeks.

Football was cited as the most traumatic sport, but soccer was second. One test of the memory of soccer players showed that after a mild head injury, 27 percent had scores that indicated an impaired performance. These results lasted for up to five days.

The real culprit seems to be repeated mild head injuries. Those who suffer one concussion seem to be at increased risk of a second injury. Even the act of repeatedly "heading" a ball in soccer can eventually cause some head trauma, especially if the ball is traveling at a high rate of speed. If you are in a sport that requires a helmet, make sure it's of the highest quality. If you are in a sport, such as soccer, that doesn't require a helmet, make sure that you report any suspected head injury to your coach or athletic trainer immediately and leave the game.

WATCH THE NECK, TOO

The most common injury to the neck is a sprain, known popularly as a stiff neck. It can happen after a quick turn or sudden movement. Symptoms are muscle spasm, stiffness, loss of motion, and pain when the neck is turned or twisted. The pain from this minor injury normally does not go down to the shoulder, arm, or back. If that happens, see a doctor. Otherwise, the suggested treatment for a neck sprain is a few days of rest with periodic application of ice and gentle stretching. An athlete can usually return to the playing field within a few days, or whenever the stiffness goes away.

More severe neck injuries can also affect the spinal cord. The most severe, of course, is a broken neck. This can result in partial or full paralysis. Any neck injury in which the athlete has trouble moving her arms or legs, or feels tingling and numbness in those parts, must be cared for immediately. Medical help should be summoned and the ath-

lete kept still. Do not move the injured athlete from the place where the injury occurred. Emergency medical technicians will immobilize the neck and put the patient on a spine board to restrict movement before transporting her to a hospital.

Another serious neck injury is whiplash. Whiplash results from sudden extension and flexion of the neck—a force causing the head to snap forward and backward. If you are hit from behind and don't see the other person coming, your neck can snap back. Even a jarring fall can cause a whiplash injury.

Whiplash is serious because it can injure the joints, ligaments, muscles, nerves, and other parts of the neck and upper back. Effects can be short-term or last for years. You may sometimes feel the pain immediately or perhaps not for several days. If you feel even the slightest neck pain after a hit or a fall, have it checked out by a physician or athletic trainer quickly. If it is determined that you have whiplash, you may be fitted with a foam-rubber neck brace. This will ease stress on the neck, which is important to healing.

The degree of the injury will determine the treatment. For mild to moderate whiplash, your doctor may prescribe a combination of heat, cold, ultrasound, massage, and gradually increasing exercises, usually monitored by a physical therapist or athletic trainer. Some doctors now believe that faster healing of whiplash is accomplished by continuing normal activities. If you are diagnosed with whiplash, follow your doctor's orders, report any continuing pain, and don't resume your sports activities until you get total medical clearance.

Injuries to the head and neck can have long-term effects if not diagnosed properly and treated quickly. Never take a chance. If you sustain any of these injuries, make sure you seek medical attention as soon as possible.

Upper-Body Injuries

Injuries to the upper body—hand, wrist, elbow, arm, or shoulder— may not be quite as numerous as other types of injuries in young girls. Yet injuries to the upper body can be serious and can put a young athlete out of action. As with any other type of injury, if you feel you have anything other than a minor bruise, tell your coach or parents and see a certified athletic trainer or physician.

GROWTH-PLATE INJURIES

The growth plate is the area of developing tissue near the ends of the long bones (as in the arms and legs) of children and adolescents. Each long bone has at least two growth plates, one at each end. These growth plates determine the future length and shape of the mature bone. When a person stops growing, the growth plates are replaced by solid bone.

Growth plates are prone to fractures because they are the weakest area of a growing skeleton. An injury that would cause a sprain in an adult may cause a serious growth-plate injury in a young person. The greatest incidence of these injuries occur in 11- to 12-year-old girls, and in 14-year-old boys. Older girls have fewer of these fractures because their bodies mature at an earlier age than boys.

Growth-plate fractures occur most often in the long bones of the fingers, followed by the outer bone of the forearm at the wrist. They can, however, also occur in the lower bones of the leg, ankle, foot, upper leg, and hip. They can be caused by a fall or blow to the body, or as the result of overuse.

If you have persistent pain in your arms or legs that is affecting your performance, and if the pain hinders your ability to move or put pressure on a limb, you should be checked by a doctor. This could be a sign of a growth-plate fracture. There are several degrees of fracture. All should be treated by an orthopedic surgeon. Treatment usually consists of the injured area being immobilized by a cast or splint. This will be left in place until the injury heals, usually for a period of a few weeks to several months.

The area of the injury will have to be rehabilitated by strength exercises, as well as exercises to help restore the full range of motion. With growth-plate fractures, long-term follow-up is recommended. Because these injuries occur in areas of continued growth, they should be monitored at three- to six-month intervals for at least two years. Some doctors prefer to continue watching the injury until the patient's bones finish growing. That way, they can be sure there is no permanent damage. Despite the need for long-term follow-up, youngsters with growth-plate fractures can usually resume their sports activities after the initial fracture has healed.

arm is still growing often presents a high risk of injury.

Medical studies show that when a player under age 14 throws more than 300 pitches a week, the likelihood of developing elbow problems increases dramatically. Doctors feel that under no circumstances should

LITTLE LEAGUE ELBOW

Little League elbow is a term that describes arm injuries to young baseball pitchers. In years past, girls played mostly softball. A softball pitcher throws underhand. This is a natural motion of the arm and less likely to result in injuries. Throwing a baseball overhand, however, is an unnatural motion. That's why so many big-league pitchers have shoulder and elbow problems, many of which require surgery. Now, many girls play baseball and throw overhand. Pitching overhand while the

Young athletes
should use moderation when pitching or throwing overhand to protect against the painful injury known as Little League elbow.

young pitchers be allowed to throw more than 300 a week. That includes games, practices, and throwing sessions at home. To protect your arm, you can get a number counter and have a friend or teammate keep track of your pitches so you don't throw more than you should.

To further keep young arms healthy, doctors suggest that kids do not try to develop a curve ball or other pitch that requires a twisting motion of the arm and wrist until they are at least 14 years of age. If you begin experiencing any arm or elbow pain while pitching, stop immediately and have your arm checked by a sports physician. Don't try to pitch through the pain, no matter how important the game, or even if your teammates and friends urge you to go on. That can make a minor injury a serious one.

SHOULDER PROBLEMS

Overuse in a number of sports can also result in shoulder problems. As with other areas of the body, injuries to the shoulder can range from minor soreness to major structural damage that requires surgery. Keeping your shoulders healthy is extremely important for athletes involved in sports that require overhead motions of the arm.

Baseball pitchers, tennis players, and swimmers are all susceptible to this type of shoulder injury. The act of serving a tennis ball can result in both shoulder and elbow injuries, especially if the server twists her wrist to put a slice or spin on the ball. As with pitching, young tennis players should not overdo it and hit too many serves in the course of a week. If you feel any arm or elbow pain, stop playing immediately and see a doctor.

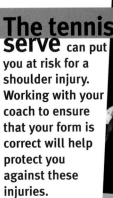

The tennis serve can put you at risk for a shoulder injury. Working with your coach to ensure that your form is correct will help protect you against these injuries.

It is thought that girls and women in competitive swimming are more prone to shoulder injuries than their male counterparts. This is because girls generally have shorter arms and shorter bodies than boys. Therefore, they must take more strokes to cover the same distance and thus put more strain on the shoulders. This situation is made even worse by the fact that girls have relatively weaker shoulder girdle muscles than boys and must work the muscles even harder.

The most common shoulder problem resulting from too much repetitive motion is called "impingement syndrome." It is more commonly known as a rotator-cuff problem. The tendons of four muscles in the shoulder form the rotator cuff. These tendons attach muscles to bones and enable the shoulder to function. Part of the shoulder blade at the roof of the shoulder is called the acromion. Between the acromion and the rotator cuff is a bursa, which allows the parts to slide against one another without much friction.

Impingement occurs when the rotator-cuff muscles are weak or do not function in a coordinated manner. This affects the head of the upper-arm bone, then rides up under the bony acromion, pinching the rest of the rotator cuff structure. The bursa sack then thickens, and the tightness is increased.

The condition produces pain and some restriction of full motion. To correct the problem, a knowledge-able athletic trainer is needed. The rotator cuff must be strengthened and the repetitive motion analyzed. You may be making some mechani-cal errors in your form, causing the repetitive motion to lead to fatigue and impingement. Proper warm-up and slowly increasing your repetitive activity will also help prevent impingement syndrome.

More serious rotator-cuff prob-lems include weakened tendons that begin to tear. Small tears in the tendons cause vague pain in the shoulder and arm. With a complete tear of the rotator cuff, you won't be able to raise your arm away from your side without pain. While partial tears will heal through rehabilitation and strengthening exercises, a com-plete tear will not heal and you will need surgery.

Young athletes involved in a sport that requires repetitive motion of the shoulder should be aware of any pain or signs of weakening. A rotator-cuff tear is a serious injury. Small tears, if ignored, can worsen. A still-growing athlete must be especially careful not to overtrain or put too much pressure on the shoul-der. It will strengthen as you become older. Make sure the mechanics of your sport are correct, and don't push yourself when you're tired.

OTHER INJURIES

Wrists are susceptible to sprains. Finger injuries include dislocations and hyperextension. Take these hurts to an athletic trainer or doctor immediately. A more minor, but common, hand injury is a blister.

Blisters are formed when the skin rubs against another surface (such as a bat, tennis racket, or lacrosse stick), causing friction. A tear occurs within the upper layers of the skin, which forms a space between the layers while leaving the surface intact. Fluid then seeps into the space. Blisters form more easily on moist skin than on dry or soaked skin. Warm weather also aids in blister formation.

When you discover a blister, you will want to relieve the pain, keep the blister from enlarging, and also prevent infection. Signs of infection include pus draining from the blister, very red or warm skin around the blister, or red streaks leading away from the blister. If you think a blister is infected, see a doctor for the proper medication.

Otherwise, the treatment isn't difficult. If the blister is small, the best protection is the blister's own skin. To protect it, just cover it with a small adhesive bandage. A larger blister should be drained without removing the protective skin. You should have this done only by your parents or an athletic trainer or doctor.

To prevent hand blisters, you can wear gloves, tape areas that are prone to blisters, or use powder or antiperspirants to help keep your hands dry. Repeated activity with the hands will cause calluses, or thickened skin, to form over areas prone to blisters.

Blisters can also form on the feet. To help prevent them, break in new shoes slowly, especially if they seem to be stiff and rubbing any area of your feet. Change socks frequently, especially if they become soaked with perspiration. Hand or foot blisters can be a painful annoyance and can hinder your performance. Prevent them if possible and seek treatment immediately if they form.

Lower-Body Injuries

The hips, legs, knees, feet, and ankles are all important for successful athletic performance. The lower body gives an athlete her speed and power in all sports. Therefore, it is extremely important to keep the lower body in tip-top shape and injury free.

STRESS FRACTURES

A stress fracture is an overuse injury that occurs when muscles become fatigued and are unable to absorb added shock. These fatigued muscles eventually transfer the overload of stress to the bone. This causes a tiny crack in the bone, known as a stress fracture.

Most stress fractures occur in the weight-bearing bones of the lower leg and foot. In fact, more than 50 percent of these injuries occur in the lower leg. They are often the result of increasing the amount or intensity of an activity too rapidly. In addition, they can be caused by the impact of an unfamiliar surface. This can happen, for example, to a tennis player who has switched from a soft to a hard court, a basketball player suddenly getting a dramatic increase in playing time, or a runner using worn or less flexible shoes. Athletes participating in tennis, track and field, gymnastics, soccer, lacrosse, field hockey, and basketball are the most susceptible to stress fractures.

A stress fracture causes pain and sometimes swelling. It can sometimes be diagnosed by an X ray, but a bone scan is the most definitive test. The most important treatment is rest—staying away from the activity that caused the fracture. Anything you do that causes pain in the area of the injury isn't good. It usually takes a stress fracture approximately six to eight weeks to heal. If you resume your sport too soon, a larger stress fracture can develop. A second stress fracture in the same place can often result in chronic problems, and the fracture may never heal properly.

Your doctor or athletic trainer can suggest strengthening and flexibility exercises to help you recover from a stress fracture. An athlete prone to lower-leg injuries and stress fractures should also have her feet checked to make sure there are no structural problems. If there are, specially designed shoes may be necessary.

Doctors advise young athletes to increase the time and intensity of their sport slowly, building up their strength and stamina. They also recommend maintaining a healthy diet and eating enough foods rich in calcium, a mineral that strengthens bones. If you have any symptoms of a stress fracture, stop your activity immediately and rest for a few days. If the pain continues, see a doctor.

KNEE INJURIES

One of the most feared injuries in sports is the knee injury. A severe knee injury is not only very painful, but it can also lead to surgery and a long rehabilitation. Knee injuries can range from a mild sprain, where rest is recommended, to a torn ligament requiring surgery. Injuries that once required major surgery, such as cartilage tears, can now be repaired using arthroscopic surgery. In this technique the surgeon fixes the tear through two small openings in the knee instead of a major incision. Recovery time is much faster.

Knee injuries occur in contact sports, in sports that require jumping, such as basketball and volley-

ball, and in sports that involve a lot of quick stops and starts as well as changes in direction. Soccer and field hockey are two such sports. As mentioned earlier, girls and women are much more susceptible to tearing the anterior cruciate ligament (ACL) in the knee. The injury can sometimes occur without warning.

"I was sprinting forward and the ball was passed out to the sideline, and I turned and went the wrong way," said soccer player Kaylee Whitfield, who suffered an ACL tear. "My knee went [one] way and I went [the other] way and it just snapped, and I fell to the ground. It was the most excruciating pain I ever felt."

If you are unfortunate enough to sustain an ACL tear, most times you will know it immediately, as Kaylee did. But there are lesser knee injuries that you should also be aware of.

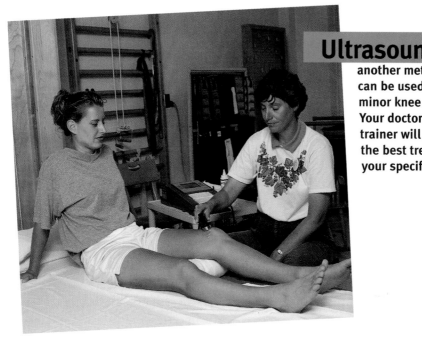

Ultrasound is another method that can be used to treat minor knee injuries. Your doctor or athletic trainer will recommend the best treatment for your specific injury.

A minor knee sprain, for instance, will not cause the knee to give way. The knee may have to be immobilized for a short time, however. Once the tear heals, you will have to stretch and strengthen the muscles to help hold the knee in place. More serious sprains can result in a complete tear in the ligament and take much longer to heal.

A twisted knee can result in a tear of the meniscus. This is the cartilage that acts as a cushion between the bones of the upper and lower leg at the knee. This type of injury can be repaired with arthroscopic surgery. Once the knee is healed, you will have to strengthen the knee under the guidance of an athletic trainer or physical therapist before you can return to action.

As with other areas of the body, report any soreness or swelling of your knees to your coach, athletic trainer, or parents. If you have any continuing pain or restriction of movement in the knee area, there may be an injury that needs attention. Don't take a chance. The knees are a vulnerable part of an athlete's body. Don't risk ignoring a minor injury that may turn into a major one.

HAMSTRING INJURIES

The hamstring muscles are located in the back of the thigh. When these muscles are subject to high tension, they can tear suddenly. Sprinters always have to be leery of hamstring injuries. Anyone in a sport that requires a quick burst of speed can also pull a hamstring.

Repeated hamstring injuries occur if a previous injury is not properly rehabilitated. They can also be the result of small amounts of trauma to the hamstring over a long period of time. Distance runners often suffer this problem. Small tears cause the hamstring to shorten and tighten. Sooner or later, this will cause a more significant strain, or tear, limiting your ability to run.

If you sustain a hamstring injury, you must rehabilitate it completely before you resume your sport. Young athletes should practice the R.I.C.E. regimen.

After that, you can begin to gently stretch the leg. An athletic trainer can show you some rehabilitation exercises to help return the full range of motion and strength to the muscle. Rehabilitation should proceed slowly and gradually. If you do too much too soon, chances are you will reinjure the muscle.

The best way to prevent a hamstring injury is to warm up properly and do a lot of stretching. You should also stretch the hamstrings again after you finish. This will keep the muscles from tightening. Some good stretches are included in the section How to Prevent Sports Injuries.

SPRAINED ANKLES

A sprained ankle is perhaps the most common injury in sports. It can occur in almost every sport. A basketball player lands awkwardly after jumping. A gymnast turns an ankle making a dismount. A field hockey player steps in a small hole in the field. A softball player stumbles while rounding a base, or turns her ankle while sliding. There are so many ways an athlete can suffer this injury that it is almost bound to happen to everyone sooner or later.

A sprain is a stretched or torn ligament. Depending on the degree of the sprain, the ligaments can tear partially or completely. Treatment usually involves a short period of immobilization, in which you shouldn't put any weight on the ankle, allowing the ligaments to heal. After that, you must begin a series of exercises to strengthen the muscles that help stabilize the ankle during activity. If the sprain is severe, a doctor may recommend a cast to immobilize it. On occasion, a very severe sprain will require surgery to help stabilize the ankle.

The R.I.C.E. therapy described earlier also applies here and for sprains to other joints in the body, such as the wrist, elbow, or knee.

ACHILLES TENDON INJURIES

The Achilles is the large tendon connecting the two major calf muscles to the back of the heel bone. If the tendon is put under too much stress, it will begin to weaken and tighten. Then, because it can't handle the stresses placed upon it, the tendon can become inflamed. At that point, the athlete has tendinitis. If this condition is not reversed, scar tissue—a product of the inflammatory process—can cover the tendon and make it even less flexible. At this stage, the tendon may tear or rupture. A rupture of the Achilles tendon is a serious injury that typically requires surgery. To come back from this surgery is a long and difficult rehabilitation.

The primary symptom of tendinitis in the Achilles is a dull or sharp pain anywhere along the back of the tendon, usually close to the heel. The ankle has less flexibility when doing calf stretches and there may be a redness over the painful area. It may also feel hot to the touch. There may also be a lumpy buildup of scar tissue that can be felt on the tendon. Sometimes you will experience a cracking sound when the ankle moves. This is scar tissue rubbing against the tendon. There may also

be some swelling, as well as pain when you point your toes or raise up on them while standing.

You can treat minor cases of Achilles tendinitis yourself. First, stop any athletic activity, and don't do any running or jumping. Ice the area for 15 to 20 minutes several times a day until the inflammation subsides. You may also massage the area of the inflammation with a heat-inducing cream or oil, but only after a physical therapist or athletic trainer has shown you the proper way to do it.

Once the inflammation goes down, you must begin to stretch the calf muscles. Don't try competing or running again until you can raise up on your toes without pain repeatedly. Begin running very gradually, and stop if you have pain. It might take six to eight weeks before you are back to easy running. If this type of Achilles tendon injury doesn't

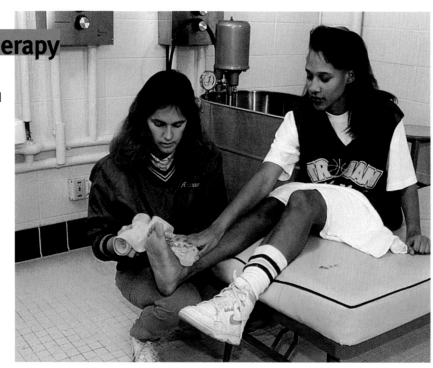

R.I.C.E. therapy can be very effective in treating a sprained ankle. Here a trainer wraps an athlete's ankle as the athlete keeps ice on the injury.

respond to treatment in two weeks, see a physical therapist or orthopedic surgeon.

Even if you have never had an Achilles tendon problem, always do stretching exercises to keep the tendon and muscles loose and flexible. A good one is to stand on the balls of your feet on a step, a curb, or a low rung on a ladder. Then drop both heels down and hold that position for a count of ten. Also strengthen and stretch the muscles in the feet and shins. The stronger the surrounding muscles, the less tension the Achilles will have to bear. An athletic trainer can outline a program that is right for you.

How to Prevent Sports Injuries

No athlete can expect to remain injury free all the time, but there are strategies that can help you minimize your risk of injury.

Here are some tips from the National Athletic Trainers' Association and the National Youth Sports Safety Foundation. They are geared to young athletes.

- Be sure your coach is certified by the national governing body of your sport or a national coaching education program.

- All suggested safety equipment in your sport should be required. You should also be sure that your equipment is properly maintained.

- Field and facilities should be maintained and inspected regularly. If this is not being done, mention it to your coach, athletic trainer, or parents.

- Make sure that you are learning all the safety rules of your sport, as well as the skills needed to participate correctly.

- There should be a "first responder" certified in first aid and CPR for emergencies at all games and practices. No one should touch or move an injured player until the first responder examines her.
- Make sure there is a first-aid kit at all games and practices.
- Fluids should always be available, and you should drink regularly during practices and games, especially in hot weather.
- Make sure your coach has an emergency information card for you and each of your teammates available at all times listing phone numbers for your parents or a close relative, as well as medical problems such as asthma, drug allergies, any medications you are taking, and diabetes. The cards should also specify allergies, such as to bee stings, foods, or poison ivy.
- Always know the location of a telephone near the facility at which you are playing. The coach should also make sure that all the players know the address where they are playing so that any one of them can direct an emergency crew to the facility.

Throughout this book, the importance of stretching muscles and tendons has been mentioned time and again. Here is one stretching routine developed for young athletes by the American Academy of Orthopaedic Surgeons. Once learned, you should take it seriously; it requires no more than ten minutes. It should be done before practice or a game, or even if you are competing informally with your friends. It will go a long way toward helping you prevent minor injuries, and perhaps some major ones as well.

1. Seat Straddle Lotus Sit down on the floor. Place the soles of your feet together and drop your knees toward the floor. Place your forearms on the inside of your knees and gently push your knees to the ground. Lean forward, bringing your chin to your feet. Hold this position for five seconds and repeat it three to six times.

2. Seat Side Straddle Sit with your legs spread. Place both your hands on the same ankle. Slowly bring your chin to your knee while keeping the leg straight. Hold for five seconds. Repeat three to six times. Alternate the exercise on opposite legs.

3. Seat Stretch Sit with your legs together, feet flexed, your hands on your ankles. Then bring your chin to your knees. Hold for five seconds and repeat three to six times.

4. Lying Quad Stretch Lie on your back with one leg straight, the other leg with hip turned in, foot facing out, and knee bent. Press your knee to the floor. Hold it five seconds and repeat three to six times before switching to the other leg.

5. Knees to Chest Lie on your back with knees bent. Grasp your knees and bring them out toward your armpits, rocking gen-tly. Hold for five seconds. Repeat three to five times.

6. Forward Lunges Stand straight. Then place your right leg forward until your knee is bent at a right angle. Lunge forward, keeping your back leg straight. The stretch should be felt on the left groin. Hold for five seconds. Repeat three to six times, then lunge forward with the other leg.

7. Side Lunges Stand with your legs apart. Bend the left knee while leaning toward the left. Keep your back straight and your right leg straight. Hold for five seconds. Repeat three to six times and then do the opposite leg.

8. Cross Over Stand with legs crossed. Keep your feet close together and your legs straight. Bend at the waist and touch your toes. Hold for five seconds. Then repeat three to six times before crossing over with the opposite leg.

9. Standing Quad Stretch Stand using your left hand to support you. Reach down with your right hand and pull your right foot to your buttocks. Hold for five seconds. Repeat three to six times before switching to the other leg.

Your coach may show you a similar stretching program, and may include additional stretches for the upper body. The more you prepare yourself for your sport, the more likely you are to avoid injury. As a rule of thumb, start slowly and increase your intensity gradually. Learn the skills of your sport so you always use the proper form. Listen to your coach and tell her or an athletic trainer about any ache or pain that worries you.

Never, under any circumstances, try to hurt someone else intentionally so that you can win. There are enough chances for an injury in sports without violating the rules of fair play. Rules exist in order to protect players from injury. And never try to play through an injury in order to win. You risk a far more serious injury, and this will hurt both your individual performance and your team in the end.

By avoiding injury you can enjoy the benefits of being an active and healthy athlete. But if you should get hurt, be smart and learn how to handle it so you can begin playing again as soon as possible.

Get in the Game!

Lots of the available resources on sports injuries are geared toward adults, but they still contain useful information. Here are some books and Web sites that will be useful if you want more information on sports injuries and their treatment and prevention.

The Complete Guide to Sports Injuries by H. Winter Griffith (New York: Berkley, 1997).

Everything You Need to Know About Sports Injuries by Lawrence Clayton (New York: Rosen, 1995).

The Sports Injury Handbook: Professional Advice for Amateur Athletes by Allen M. Levy and Mark L. Fuerst (New York: John Wiley & Sons, 1993).

Sports Injury Management by Marcia K. Anderson and Susan Hall (Philadelphia: Williams & Wilkins, 1999).

The Sports Medicine Bible: Prevent, Detect, and Treat Your Sports Injuries Through the Latest Medical Technologies by Lyle J. Micheli with Mark Jenkins (New York: HarperCollins, 1995).

kidshealth.org/parent/index.html Click on the "Kids" or "Teens" link for some excellent sports injury and health information.

www.exercise.about.com This page has many links to information about sports injuries, prevention, and health.

www.sportsparents.com/medical/sportsrx6.html Although this site is geared toward parents, it contains lots of interesting, accessible information for young people.

www.womenssportsfoundation.org A good resource for everything you want to know about women in sports, including lots of information on health and fitness.

Index